For our families — AGM & NN

Text copyright © 2016 by Acree Graham Macam
Illustrations copyright © 2016 by Natalie Nelson
Published in Canada and the USA in 2016 by Groundwood Books

Groundwood Books / House of Anansi Press
groundwoodbooks.com

With the participation of the Government of Canada
Avec la participation du gouvernement du Canada | Canadä

Library and Archives Canada Cataloguing in Publication
Macam, Acree Graham, author
The king of the birds / Acree Graham Macam ; pictures by Natalie Nelson.
Issued in print and electronic formats.
ISBN 978-1-55498-851-8 (bound). — ISBN 978-1-55498-852-5 (pdf)
I. Nelson, Natalie, illustrator  II. Title.
PZ7.1.N45Ki 2016          j813'.6          C2015-908425-3
C2015-908426-1

The art for this book is composed of hand-painted paper, drawings and found photography, compiled digitally into collage.
Design by Michael Solomon
Printed and bound in Malaysia

FSC
MIX
Paper from responsible sources
FSC® C012700

# THE KING OF THE BIRDS

## ACREE GRAHAM MACAM

*pictures by*
## NATALIE NELSON

 GROUNDWOOD BOOKS   HOUSE OF ANANSI PRESS   TORONTO   BERKELEY

It ALL STARTED with a chicken who could walk backwards

and forwards.

A newspaperman came from New York to see the chicken, and Flannery became famous.

But not long after, people forgot about Flannery. And she began to feel that life was a little too quiet.

More birds would do the trick. She collected her savings and bought one of every type she could find.

They were a big help around the house.

"You think you got enough birds?"
the boy from next door asked.
Flannery shrugged. "Not really."
Life was still a little too quiet.

A peacock would be more exciting than a thousand birds! Flannery had to have one.

She did extra chores for a week to convince her mother.

At the train station, Flannery recognized the peacock instantly.

"That's him!" she cried, racing down the platform.

The peacock was equally enthused.

"HE'S IN CHARGE NOW,"

she told the rest of the birds when she arrived home from the train station.

The peacock took a
strut around, sizing up
his kingdom.

But he already knew — life here
was a little too quiet.

"What's wrong with him?" the boy from next door asked one day. "Isn't he supposed to have a tail?"

"He does have a tail," said Flannery. "It's just that he only fans it when he feels like it."

But the truth was, he never had felt like it.
At least not in front of Flannery.
And she had done everything she could to
get him to.

She threw him a party.

She let him play in the fig tree.

She fed him a feast of flowers.

And she staged a parade in his honor.
But he wouldn't lift a feather of that tail, even
though he seemed to enjoy the attention.

QUA!
QUA! QUA!
QUA!
QUA! QUA!
QUA!

MRAW

One night, Flannery awoke to a horrible noise.

She shot up in bed. "I know."

The next afternoon she gathered her collection for an important announcement.

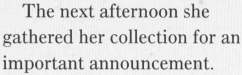

"**I HEREBY** *introduce* THE **QUEEN** OF THE **BIRDS**."

She plopped the new peahen down onto the ground.

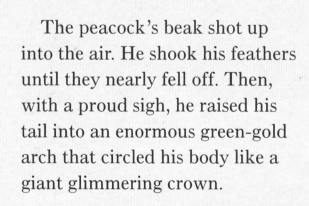

The peacock's beak shot up into the air. He shook his feathers until they nearly fell off. Then, with a proud sigh, he raised his tail into an enormous green-gold arch that circled his body like a giant glimmering crown.

The queen looked down at the ground,
interested in some rocks that were there.

The neighbors, however, flocked to witness
the peacock's amazing crown.
"Wonderful," they gasped.

But the boy from next door was still not impressed. He screwed up his face like he smelled something funny and pointed at the queen.

"Where's *her* crown?"

"Where's yours?" Flannery retorted.

The boy huffed off home, the queen headed back to the pen, and the peacock followed, strutting like he'd never strutted before.

Flannery took up the rear like a royal attendant.

The king and queen of the birds almost lived happily ever after.

But life, they felt, was still a little too quiet...

THIS STORY WAS INSPIRED by the life and writings of Flannery O'Connor, who was born in Georgia in 1925 and departed our world at the age of thirty-nine, surrounded by her collection of ducks, swans, guinea hens and — of course — peacocks.

The real Flannery described her young self as a "pigeon-toed child with a receding chin and a you-leave-me-alone-or-I'll-bite-you complex." When Flannery was six, she really did appear in the news because of a chicken she had trained to walk backwards.

Ms. O'Connor and her "I'll-bite-you complex" went on to write stories that un-hid people's ugly, mean parts and proved that everybody — even preachers and grandmothers — needs to be forgiven.

When you are older, go read "A Good Man Is Hard to Find," and let us know what you think.

Acree & Natalie